A MODERN SHIVA STORY

BLIND

PREETI C. SHARMA WRITING AS
MARAH DEVI

TEACUP PUBLISHING

Blind

Copyright © 2021 by Preeti C. Sharma

All rights reserved. No part of this publication may be reproduced, distributed, or transmitted in any form or by any means, electronic or mechanical, including photocopying, recording, or by any other information storage and retrieval system without the prior written permission of the publisher, except in brief quotations embodied in critical reviews and certain other noncommercial uses permitted by copyright law.

This book is a work of fiction. Any resemblance to real people, living or dead, events, or locales is purely coincidental. All names, characters, places, and incidents in this work are figments of the author's imagination or are used fictitiously.

Cover Illustration by Preeti C. Sharma from the following images:

Akhilan. Azhimala Siva Statue January 2020, CC BY-SA 4.0, via Wikimedia Commons
Snap2objects.com. Cityscapes Vectors, CC by 4.0, via FreeVector.com

It's dawn on my favorite mountain, and I can still feel *her* with me. Has another lifetime passed for her so we can meet again?

Deepening the bend in my elbows, I allow my muscles to burn more as I hold my legs wrapped around my right bicep. Eight-angle pose, the hot yoga enthusiasts call it. Given that I have been meditating in these poses on Mount Kailash—in the snow, the freezing streams, in the heat of the summer—since before the beginning of time, the idea that they want to turn up the heat in their little buildings for an hour-long class makes me laugh. I remember Astavakra, for whom they named the pose—clearly, though he attained salvation ... was it in another, earlier universe or this one? Unchecked ego caused his own father to curse him with deformities while he was yet in the womb, but Astravakra sought to right his father's sins even so.

Anyway, ensuing centuries have still not taught humans that age and enlightenment are seldom connected. Sometimes sages like Astavakra join me, and sometimes pilgrims who suspect the truth of who I am do find their way to my mountain. They are all welcome, so long as their hearts hold pure intent. I remember a time when my beloved proved her identity by meditating for years at a time.

Her goat's ass of a father, back when she was Shakti ... no, I can't let myself recall the memory. It angers me, and when you control the power of destruction, getting angry doesn't work out well for the universe. I focus on the breath of the universe until the destructive edge that plagues me fades to nothing.

Still, it's time I find Parvati again, but the ghosts and imps across the world have nothing to report. Except—

"Supreme Lord, a demon has been stalking the women's shelter of the Holy Mother."

I unwind my legs, press up into a handstand, then return to standing before responding. Not that his words warrant a verbal response. I know where this demon is, though Parvati has built shelters across the globe for battered women and homeless children.

"O Great Illuminator?" Nandi asks. From his seat beside me, where he watches over me and meditates, he lumbers to his four legs with a grace absent in mortal cattle. Nandi finds pleasure in greeting me with a different epithet each time, though he lacks the ego to call me the Lord Whose Vehicle is a Bull. He, after all, is that bull. "May I transport you?"

"That demon needs killing," I mutter. No one infringes on my lady's projects without paying the price. And if he actually harmed any one of those women, I'll make sure he regrets it for what remains of his miserable existence.

Sometimes I hate reincarnation. The demons come back just as well as the rest. Each turn of life takes my beloved from me, takes the other deities away, to start anew. I alone remain eternal and beyond the cycle of birth and death. Being unending can be lonely, as I am the only one who has seen every moment in every universe, who has watched each light wink out and every breath fade.

But with hope of seeing her again now, I may as well find out just who this demon is. If he's my responsibility—not one for an avatar—I don't want to dawdle. I prefer to spend my efforts looking for Parvati, to maximize the time we have together in her current incarnation.

I'm not sure why she chooses rebirth as an avatar again and again, when she could simply take her immortal form and stay by my side forever. Even Vishnu, the one I count as my truest friend, likes to take human forms, to inspire humans with the promise of salvation. Rama, Krishna, Buddha, and I can't remember the name of the latest version of himself. He prefers to act rather than observe, as I do. Too much action from one such as me has never helped this creation.

If I couldn't recognize the avatars in their astral forms in every rebirth, I would find myself truly alone ... more alone than I already am, surrounded by the changeable, the mortal, the impermanent. I have known more loneliness than any other being, for I am the only infinite, the only forever.

Vishnu would be happy to help me tracking the demon, but I don't want to bother him. His human form is too fragile, anyway, even if the weapon I gifted him holds more power than any other that has ever or will ever exist. For now, I will handle the demon myself.

In a blink, I transport from Mount Kailash through the astral plane and find myself in front of the shelter disguised as a homeless man. I circle the shelter and the rest of the block while pretending to beg. This particular guise is so repulsive, with its unwashed stench and matted hair, that no one spares me a single coin. The people crossing my path avoid my form, just as I wished it. Still, it stings that in this particular moment and in this precise place, no one offers compassion or even a kind smile. Those who may have wanted to offer something still suspected I would only squander their charity.

I guess it's really only a face Parvati could love, though she actually told me off in this form for speaking ill of her beloved Shiva. The bright snap of her eyes, the righteous fury filling her form as she reprimanded him—no one defended more vigorously than my lady. As a mortal princess, more beautiful in her soul than her body, she sacrificed her happiness to wait upon me during the long darkness that plagued me after Shakti had been ripped from me. Her only wish amidst all her dedicated devotion was to marry me, who turned her away and ignored her and refused to acknowledge either her love or the incomparable extremes of her meditation and fasts.

I still don't know what she saw in me then, what she sees in me in any of her many reincarnations, that makes me worthy of her love. I am grateful for her unmatched sacrifice and the purity of her boundless love.

After a few more steps forward on the rapidly emptying sidewalk, I sense it. Evil emanates from the demon's aura before I spot him. Sending out a single pulse of demand, a platoon of ghosts and imps materialize before me. "Track that demon, and make sure he doesn't see you. I want to know his schedule, who he reports to, and what he's doing. If you catch a glimpse of my lady, tell me at once. If someone is in imminent danger because of him, summon me immediately."

My soldiers bow their heads and disperse, some through the astral plane and others through sidewalk cracks and gutters. I shift back to Mount Kailash, returning to my regular form. My skin, despite long exposure to the sun and the elements, remains pale. Perhaps all the ashes in the cremation grounds has stayed upon me from when I smeared them on my skin. Everything, except me, must die and eventually turn to nothing more than ash.

The crescent moon adorns my matted hair, which sits on the top of my head coiled into a horn or a shell—not like a unicorn, more like a hill. A string of prayer beads rests on my chest, and Vasuki, king of snakes, garlands my neck. My chosen weapons are never far—the trident Trishula, the axe, and the small hourglass-shaped drum. Deceptively innocuous, the damaru might be the most dangerous of the three. I harness its power when I dance, and some of my dances have destroyed universes.

Here on my chosen mountain, I await the soldiers' reports and check the rest of the sustainable farms, soup kitchens, orphanages, and schools Parvati has set up over the course of her many lifetimes. Some gods may choose to utilize modern technology. While the internet has its uses, meditation attunes me instantaneously to whatever I seek. Why hunch over a keyboard when I can complete my investigation in crow pose? The list of facilities seems endless, even to one who is infinite, and no one has anything of note to tell me.

Finally the platoon following the demon begins to trickle in.

"Faultless One, I cleared the obscene poetry he printed and taped on every window and in every mailbox...."

"Lord of the Universe, I scrubbed clean the graffiti he left on the building and in the parking garage...."

"Giver of Joy, I restored the power he cut as soon as the others distracted him...."

"Auspicious One, I buried the dead animals he left on the doorstep...."

I almost blink at that one. It is the work of but a moment's thought to free the souls of those creatures and grant them eternal salvation.

"Supreme Teacher, I diverted all his phone calls to the shelter to dial the cell phones of scammers targeting senior citizens ...."

"Creator, I disabled the speakers of his car when he blasted the music on the street in the early morning ...."

"Lord of Time, I put chiggers in his shoes and bedbugs in his underwear drawer ...."

Imps, honestly ....

"Ever-Radiant One, I disposed of the box of dead roses he mailed ...."

So the list goes on until they all report.

"Good work, all of you," I tell them. They provided more than enough evidence for me to act. I leave my mountain for the women's shelter again, shifting into the worldly plane and taking the guise of a clueless interviewee, complete with a neat but ill-fitting business suit and a vacant expression. None will question my presence until I loop the block a second time, but I don't even reach the intersection before finding the demon.

He lounges in the patio seat of a cafe, sipping an overpriced drink and reading the newspaper, looking for all the world like mid-level management. Which in some sense, I suppose he is. But on a closer look, he looks familiar—a minion ... for one of my greatest regrets.

Parvati playfully covered my eyes one day while I was meditating, as if she could sneak up on me. For that single moment that she blocked my vision, the astral world fell dark. Parvati—along with the rest of the universe—freaked out. Sweat dripped from her clammy palms, giving birth to Andhaka, a baby blind in both the astral and worldly planes. Is he our kid? I mean ... there are stranger ways gods and demons have come to life, but no one can argue that he is only alive—that he was only created—through our actions.

In her last life, Parvati found him an adoptive family. They called him "Andy," and he got a top-notch education and just about every luxury a kid could wish for. But his greed and his ego—for he was born a demon—means that nothing was ever enough for him. Now a grown man, his strength combined with his demon wiles made him heir to quite a fortune, with no suspicion falling upon him.

If his minion is here, where is Andhaka? No matter, I still need to dispose of this minion.

A look around the area doesn't reveal any obvious ways to dispose of him. *How tiresome.* Snapping back into the homeless beggar form I used before, I shuffle over, drawing just enough attention that people deliberately evade my gaze. So when I drop to a seat on the sidewalk, leaning against the pickets of the cafe's black aluminum fence, I'm right next to the demon.

His nostrils flare, and he turns his head to peer at me over the edge of his newspaper. "You mind?" he snarled.

I meet his stare. He folds his paper in disgust, setting it on the table as he prepares to leave.

Perfect. Before he stands, I reach within and open my third eye. Recognition flashes in his eyes before I burn him to ash that wafts into the graveled landscaping. Shifting my appearance once more, I grab his wallet and cellphone from the chair. The table looks like someone abandoned their paper and was too lazy to dump their used cup in the trash. Meanwhile, I look like a spry septuagenarian: capable, wealthy, but physically harmless. This guise usually leaves people eager to hold doors and speak a little louder than necessary, but they certainly won't question any eccentricities.

I open the billfold, finding several large bills but no credit cards or ID. The cellphone contact list yields more fruit—a number for one Andy. I'll call him, but first I need to check on the shelter.

Two sharp knocks and a reference to one of the many charities I finance gets me in the door. A name and a face famous for philanthropic efforts can help in these situations. Obviously I fund homeless shelters and sponsor refugees hand-in-hand with Parvati's foundations. Well-known scientists also tout my efforts to save endangered species. Humans are doing a great job of destroying this planet without my assistance. Considering I hunted tigers and elephants in another lifetime, eons ago now, it seems strange that I must now speak up for their survival. I still wear that tiger hide, and the elephant's head replaced my son's after an unfortunate misunderstanding with Parvati.

Here, at this women's shelter, the large donation of the demon's cash I drop in the envelope I ask for leaves both the receptionist and the security guard suitably impressed. Under the chemical odor of industrial cleaners and decades apart, I can still catch the scent of *her* being. Her protection permeates this building and the people within it, much like the bulletproof glass separating visitors from authorized personnel.

My gaze falls on a portrait on the wall in pride of place. Her hair is gray, and wrinkles punctuate her eyes and divide her brow. But the serene expression she wears, the gentle warmth in her deep brown eyes—I recognize those across every lifetime. I incline my head to the ornate frame. "I knew Uma, mostly by reputation"—a small mistruth to keep their suspicions at bay—"but I haven't met her replacement yet."

"She'll be so disappointed she missed you, sir." I notice she doesn't offer a name for Uma's new form. The receptionist's firm voice also holds a tinge of false regret. She's lying, but I silently commend her for protecting my beloved.

But does that mean Parvati is here? Now? I have to thwart this gatekeeper to find out.

"Could you make an appointment for us to meet?" I don't care if she's lying to protect Parvati from those who might harass a woman operating a women's shelter or if Parvati has issued orders not to be interrupted. At that possibility, I have to stifle a snort. The last time Parvati tried to bar my entry to our home, she didn't care for the consequences. At least we have a wonderful son to show for it. And I suppose I learned that she deserves her privacy.

However, she will also want to know of my presence, that we have found each other once more in this lifetime. If Parvati is here, I just have to stall long enough to catch her notice. Instead of just moving through the astral plane into her presence as I might have before the incident with Ganesha, I will wait here respectfully until she has time for me. I have nowhere else I need to be. Of course, I can also speed things along without getting anyone—including myself—in trouble for denying her wishes.

"Are there any specific items the shelter particularly needs?" I pull a notepad and pen from my blazer's inner pocket to show my interest. The reading glasses perched on my nose help, but I need to complete the picture. A dry cough erupts from my chest, wracking the frail body. I maintain the pretense until the receptionist offers me a glass of water. When she rises and leaves for the inner room, the volume of my hacking cough increases, certain to be heard in the large office within.

Sure enough, a vision of perfection emerges. I barely register the sensible outfit draping her physical form— for her astral self shines brighter than any star.

Parvati's eyes widen in joy and shock when she sees me, but she restrains herself in front of her staff. Need and love radiate from her very essence, her astral arms already reaching for me. "Please, won't you take a seat in my office? It's such an honor that you made time to visit us." Even now, her first words to me see to my comfort and show her everlasting worship. Her staff might only hear the politeness due a benefactor, but I know better. Parvati sacrificed every worldly advantage to meditate on my name in hopes that I might grant her the dearest wish of her heart. I was an angry, bitter fool to resist her for as long as I did. How lost was I in my grief that I did not recognize Shakti reborn in Parvati?

Parvati rushes to open the door, her hand reaching for my elbow as if to convince herself that I truly stand before her. I relish the touch, even through the many layers of fabric separating us, before I hold the door open and wait for her to precede me. She ushers me into her office, closing the door firmly behind her and locking it for good measure.

I take in the details of her office with a distracted glance: her scarred wooden desk, with two computer monitors, is the same one she used in a previous life. Its side presses against one wall so she can sit facing the door. Across the back wall, a bookshelf stands full of women's memoirs and counseling texts. Two well-maintained leather chairs sit angled to her desk, and the remaining wall holds an inviting sofa that wasn't there on my last visit. Nothing in the space screams of wealth or extravagance: Parvati uses her resources to benefit her devotees, not to bring herself comfort.

Parvati turns toward me. Only then do I let myself look upon her true self—her face is resplendent with light and love, her nubile body as perfect and desirable as I remember it. My body has only ever desired hers. My hands have traveled every curve and surface. I know her form even better than I know my own, and I'm impatient to do so again. Her hungry gaze looks at me with the same need, and we embrace there in the astral plane, the light of our forms merging together to rival ten million suns. We could stay like that forever, but the workers at the shelter will eventually grow suspicious.

The interruption that forces us apart comes from Nandi, though. How did he get past the receptionist? Was she so nonplussed that a white bull wandered in and started talking to her that she just let him in? Then I realize that he has come to us in the astral plane.

His horns tip toward the ground as he speaks to me, clearly too embarrassed at the sight of us together to meet my eyes. We're not even in a compromising position—while we both cup each other's faces with one pair of hands, the other set of our arms encircle each other, *outside* our garments. Parvati's white sari, trimmed in gold, covers rather more of her body than the tiger skin I wear, but it's no big deal. Nandi has walked in on us doing far more. Half the pantheon has walked in on us doing more—and some claim as many as three hundred thirty million Hindu gods. A ridiculous but amusing misinterpretation .... After all, there is only one supreme power.

"Moon-Crested One, the Lord of the Senses seeks your aid." There was no question that Nandi meant *now*.

Vishnu has never asked such a thing idly. What could have gone so badly wrong so quickly that he didn't speak to me himself? Perhaps my earlier resistance to asking him to join me occurred because I sensed his preoccupation. Still, his needing my help spoke of trouble.

"Very well. Tell him I'm on my way." I must attend to one matter first. Reaching back to the human world, I fold my consciousness around Parvati's shelter, circling the property and identifying each soul within it.

I place a benediction upon each of them. Each of the victimized women who sought refuge at Parvati's hands will now attain their salvation when they come to the end of their lifetimes. Further, none will be able to harm them with my protection upon them. The demons can send who they like—but they will fail to break the barriers I have erected.

Parvati's almond eyes widen in appreciation. "That was very generous."

I shrug off her praise. "They suffered enough." And while some of them still risk temptation, falling back into the very situations they tried to escape by seeking out the shelter, this protection will ease their path to better choices.

Squeezing two of her hands in mine, I incline my head regretfully. "I prefer to stay with you, but duty calls. Await my swift return here, my love."

Parvati smiles weakly, as loath to let go of me as I am to leave. The feel of her skin against mine fades as I shift through the astral plane in search of Vishnu. She can find me now again as easily as I can find her, but this impermanent separation still stings.

Sharp wind whips through my coiled hair. Rain pelts my skin. The cobra around my neck hisses in displeasure. Even Ganga, her waters twisting around my skull, seems frenzied. Less than half a breath steadies my thoughts once more so that I can take in the scene around me. Vishnu and the minor gods battle an army of demons across an ocean that rages under a malevolent typhoon. A heavy fog lifts from the water despite the needles of rain over the battlefield. Vishnu catches sight of me, bowing his head in gratitude and saying as much. He looks pale and dizzy, and his army fares no better. I know the power of the weapon at his disposal, so if his warriors are falling, this situation is dire indeed.

"I swear I was trying to make peace with the demons," he gasps out between choked coughs.

Of course he was. "So it didn't go according to plan?" I ask, unable to hide the amusement in my tone. How many times has he made this attempt, only to fail? I lost count long ago. I guess that his efforts inspire the humans, especially since he so often chooses a human shape and takes his battles to earth. He offers them something to believe in a form that they can understand, whether as a divine infant, a mischievous son, a loyal brother, a handsome cowherd, a faithful lover, or a noble king. If they find his form as a wandering ascetic relatable, how can I judge without hypocrisy?

Vishnu waves a weak hand at the fog, and his dusky blue skin reddens where he touches it. He tries to speak again, but he can't take in enough breath for even a whisper. This situation is very bad, to bring low so powerful a warrior.

My fingers reach out to touch the smoky wisps swirling about us and making the demon army harder to see. *Poison*, I realize, and one strong enough to harm all of them ... all of *us*.

Well, if there must be a sacrifice, I prefer not to take down all of this universe with me. Its end remains a while off, yet. Only I have any hope of containing the poison before it takes everything in its path. I reach out my hand, gently pushing Vishnu aside, and call the deadly haze toward me. It swirls and floats, finally settling in my palm as a small sip of concentrated death.

"Cheers," I mutter, even as the battle recommences around me. Vishnu bows his head in respectful resignation, readying his power to come to my aid. In a single mouthful, I swallow the toxin.

Fire fills me, and it takes all of my concentration to comprehend the agony and contain it to only my form.

Parvati is screaming. How did she get here? And where did Vishnu go? I expected to find him at my side, not my beloved. Her crossed legs cradle my head, and two of her arms have nearly pulled my entire chest onto her lap. Her other pair of hands, however, crush my throat, choking me ... at total odds with her words. "You can't die," she sobs. "You're eternal. You existed before time ... You can't die ..."

Her meaning penetrates the burn permeating my body, radiating outward from my throat. I couldn't swallow ... couldn't move this viscous fire from where it lodged ... couldn't find my voice to reassure her. Hearing her fear and panic hurt my heart in a way that I haven't felt since that terrible day in Daksha's great hall, when Shakti argued with him about slighting me. She was so offended on my behalf that she cast her body into the fire, immolating herself to defend her choice of a husband. I didn't deserve such loyalty from her then, and I don't deserve her tears now.

I don't recall what happened to Daksha's palace. The memory remains shrouded in a haze of grief and disbelief. I only remember holding her lifeless figure in my arms and weeping like a lost child. If that universe survived, it was not because of my restraint. What was I, without my other half? Incomplete, inadequate, and alone ... so painfully, irrevocably alone. She, who accepted me when I came to wed her covered in ash and little else, with a procession of ghosts and spirits, riding on a bull ... What princess, what goddess deserved an outsider such as me for a partner? But she only wanted me, and then she sacrificed her life because her father disrespected me.

After the gods made their sacrifices and forced me to part with Shakti's corpse, I fled for Mount Kailash—for the one place where I could escape the horrors my life had become. Centuries passed in a blur of yoga and meditation under the harshest of conditions.

Parvati's desperate voice penetrates the flood of my memories.

I can't leave her alone, not like she once left me. I have to answer her call.

Her divine form glows with the light of a thousand stars, and her attention focuses, laser-like, on the knot of venom in my throat. Parvati's tears stream down her cheeks, cooling as they rain down on my face ... my neck ... almost like snowflakes wandering on the breeze on the mountaintop. And those tears ease the burning in my throat, enough for me to take one great gasping breath. The very air filling my lungs reeks of the poison, but the oxygen is precious. I must find a way to comfort Parvati.

Her soft fingers brush the hair from my temple, carefully twisting it into the matted braids coiled atop my head. Her gentle touch inflames me with the need to possess her. Obviously not the time or the place, but I can't help the way my body always yearns for her. Some choose to worship us that way, either entwined forever in a single form, half-male and half-female, or the simpler and more obvious evidence of our union.

With a conscious effort, I look up at her, reaching a hand to cup her chin. I want nothing more than to kiss her now, but I dare not risk the poison touching her lips. What I can hold in my throat, despite the fiery clawing, will surely destroy her in this form. I can't lose her yet.

"My love," I rasp. She's still crushing my neck in a desperate choke. The hoarseness in my voice will hardly reassure her, but it's the best I can do for now. "Do not mourn me. I'm right here, with you, forever. No mere poison can destroy what I am or my love for you." Well, at least she now knows the poison doesn't block my throat chakra. I have no problem telling her the truths of my very being. With every word it becomes easier to speak around the poison until it becomes just another aspect of who I am. I feel a harsh bruise where the poison settled, unable to travel up or down my body thanks to the tourniquet of Parvati's hands. Is she able to neutralize the poison because Parvati's own power is the antidote for anything that ails me?

I fall into a meditative, healing state while contemplating this question. When I return to the worldly plane, the poison just another part of me, it takes a moment before I recognize where I am.

To say Parvati is displeased with me may be an understatement. But tears still glitter in her eyes. With Nandi's help, she hauled me through the astral plane back to her office, now in a different, younger guise. Apparently deciding that three's a crowd, Nandi quietly took his leave while I was resting. I'm reclining on her sofa, which is every bit as soft as it looked earlier.

She must have been waiting for me to settle on one of the planes before speaking.

"I cannot believe you drank a poison capable of killing every god and demon in existence," she storms. Parvati in a temper is magnificent, and I take a moment to admire her passion and ferocity before I answer.

"Not *every* god." I gently correct her. Nothing can truly kill me—for I have existed before any other. But the right sort of harm done to me could destroy this universe. Time could fade once more and only return when my power manifests again. Parvati has every right to be upset—if only because the poison might have separated us in this incarnation of the universe. But I also could not let the others die—not Vishnu nor even Brahma, not the lesser gods nor even the demons whose lust for power and possessions drives the endless battle between good and evil. I couldn't let all of them die.

"If your power goes to sustaining you instead of this universe, I'm pretty sure we would all be reduced to nothing." Parvati's scathing retort startles me. I didn't realize I'd spoken aloud. Or maybe I didn't—she is the other half of me. She hears what is written in my heart.

"You're right, of course, my dear," comes my droll reply, and we both look at each other and let our disagreement fade away.

"So how did you find me so quickly?" Parvati asks, just as she does every time we reunite.

"I must confess I had some demonic help with that." At her arched brow, I continue: "Andhaka's minion was staking out this building."

"Andhaka?" Parvati blinks. "I haven't heard his name in ... what's it been? Three, four decades?"

In her last human form, she barely reached middle age when she found a home for the blind baby. I assigned one of my many ghosts to track him. In their last report to me, Andhaka—Andy—inherited his parents' considerable fortune. Perhaps it was an oversight not to keep more frequent tabs on him. But I can remedy that right now.

I pat my pockets. "Where's the cell phone I brought with me earlier?"

Parvati pulls it from her drawer. I see a flash of her power before she hands it to me fully charged.

"Clever trick, my love," I murmur as I scroll through the contacts again.

The text log shows a sickening exchange. The minion was sending "Andy" pictures of my beloved in stolen everyday moments, and "Andy" waxed disturbingly, crudely poetic about her beauty and his desire to possess her.

"Beloved, he's targeting *you*, not someone at the shelter." I show her the string of messages.

"Wasn't Andhaka born blind?" Parvati asks. "Are you certain this Andy is Andhaka?"

"One way to find out." My finger hovers over the "call" icon.

"Where have you been?" a cultured voice demands.

"I thought you'd like to know that she has a boyfriend," I say, perfectly mimicking the demon from the cafe. They don't call me "the lord of great illusions" for nothing.

"Who is he?" He pauses. "Actually, I don't care. Kill him. Then I'll swoop in to comfort her."

"Why do you care so much, boss? Plenty of other fish in the sea."

"Sure there are, and I've enjoyed a few. But she and I—we're connected."

I exchange glances with Parvati, waiting for Andy to elaborate.

"I found her after I went to the lawyer who finished the paperwork, which led me to the adoption agency, which lists her as the head of the board. Funny enough, she's also the chair of women's shelters, soup kitchens, and other do-good organizations across the world. There's pictures of her working in all of them, shaking hands and kissing babies, but no record of how she got there. She even heads some support groups for nursing mothers. But before her name just appeared on all of that, I can't find her name anywhere. It's like she appeared out of nowhere, and suddenly she's bloody Mother Teresa. She's like me, and I want her."

My voice is hard as I respond, dropping any pretense of subservience to Andhaka. "Then it's too bad that she isn't interested. And for the record, she's nothing like you at all."

"Who the hell is this?" Andhaka snaps. "You don't know what I am or what she is. I'm your worst nightmare."

"Actually, I know exactly what you are, demon," I answer. "Don't concern yourself with who *she* is."

"Is she with you? And what did you do with Bali? How did you get his phone?"

"If Bali was the one staking out the women's shelter, he's no longer in your employ," I reply.

It takes him a moment, but he makes the connection. "Who are you?" he repeats. "I'll kill *you*, too."

Mighty words from someone who hides behind his minions. "You can try, but none have succeeded before," I sneer. "Those wiser than you call me 'Lord of the Gods.' Find me on Mount Kailash. I'll be waiting."

I end the call and face Parvati, preparing for an argument. She isn't going to like what I'm about to say. "I don't want you involved. He's a monster. He's going to come after me. Let him."

She rolls her eyes at me. "Do you forget who I am?"

How can I? She is my other half. Kali—*Great* Kali, Mahakali—though she is the Mother Goddess, she also commands the powers of death and destruction. She has killed demons with unmatched ferocity. In her armed form as Kali, she even wears a prayer necklace of their skulls to prove it. I needn't worry—but I still do—that she can keep herself and others safe. She protected others and went into battle more times than I care to recall.

But the malevolence in his voice ... the way that he describes his lust for her ... I would feel the urge to protect *anyone* from him, let alone my beloved.

"Then let us return to Mount Kailash and face him together." I make the compromise, but I like nothing about it. A gentle touch on my hand conveys her thoughts. She knows how I feel but appreciates that I also respect her wishes. She values the protection I offer but feels equally responsible for Andhaka.

So we shift through the astral plane, finding our way back to my mountain. We seat ourselves on flat rocks and begin to meditate. I search the astral plane for any sign of Andhaka or his minions. Nights bleed into days, finding nothing. It is Nandi's panicked voice urging me to respond.

"Imperishable One, he has taken her," Nandi whispers. "I have just returned and she is gone."

After turning to look at the empty space Parvati so lately occupied, I stare at my faithful guard, uncomprehending. I should have sensed anyone coming near us in the course of my meditation. Now that I have seen her physical form in this life, I should be able to find her anywhere again. But my desperately seeking her through the astral plane turns up nothing but an unpleasant discovery.

Given his nature and the circumstances of his birth, I can't see Andhaka or his spawn in the astral plane. He can even cloak Parvati with his demonic aura. What fresh chaos is this? Demons and their damned reincarnation ... How did he even come upon such a valuable power?

"Brahma!" my voice summons the god immediately. We two have never gotten along, but I don't believe he would actively work against me, either. "When will you stop offering ridiculous boons to demons? This one has now abducted Parvati."

Brahma looks at the ground, abashed, but he knew exactly who I meant. "I made sure there was a loophole, Faultless One." Did he pick that epithet on purpose to mock me? I digress. His simple insults do not matter. "You are the only one who can kill him." He waves his hand to show me a scene from moments before Andhaka snatches Parvati.

Brahma and Andhaka stand together, hidden from view as they observe ... us. And such is the demon's power that I could not sense either of them while they stood on *my mountain.*

The god is speaking. "It was a mistake to return your sight. You use your eyes, but you do not truly see what is before you. Do you not recognize your own parents?" Brahma inclines his head to our meditating forms. "There sit the Supreme Lord and the Holy Mother. The sweat that formed on her hands, when she covered his eyes and the world went dark, created you."

Andhaka rolls his eyes. "I know how the birds and the bees work, and that's not it. He's just a sage meditating for a boon, like I once did." He leers at Parvati. "Besides, I could do a lot better than make her palms wet."

24

Brahma shakes his head. "You've created an army of demons from drops of your own blood. You can shift through the astral plane. Why do you doubt what I tell you?"

"There's no way that woman is my mother—I'm older than she is," Andhaka insists.

Brahma frowns, clearly confused that Andhaka doesn't see the blinding aura emanating from Parvati's godly form as she meditates. They speak of the light of ten million suns glowing from Ganesha, so with what awesome power does his mother shine?

But Andhaka isn't done. "If that man killed my general, I will have my revenge. It's his fault for standing in the way of what I want. I can offer her a world of luxury that filthy cave-dweller can only dream of."

Brahma decides not to keep arguing with the demon. It is possibly the first intelligent choice he's made regarding Andhaka. "I would be careful who you choose to insult."

"I *will* have her," Andhaka says. "No one can stop me, least of all a naked man standing in a half-frozen stream. What's he going to do, 'Om' me to death?" He snorts. "It's his fault, anyway. He's standing in my path, and you *promised* me ...."

Brahma looks even more troubled. "Shall I remind you of the terms of our deal? You are not immortal—though only Shiva can kill you. And he will be motivated to do so should you attempt to defile his goddess."

"'Defile' ... you're so dramatic," Andhaka dismisses. "She'll beg for it. I'll make it so good for her that she won't want to leave my bed."

A snarl rises in my throat, and Brahma wisely ends the memory. "Is there anything I can do to help?" he asks, contrite.

"I think you've done enough." Without another word, I shift into the astral plane. Dealings with Brahma never improve. Not since the beginning, when he and Vishnu argued about which of the two of them was the superior god. So what to do except present a challenge to settle their disagreement? A burning pillar appeared before them, so Vishnu turned into a boar and started clawing for the lowest point, while Brahma took the form of a goose to fly to the top. While Vishnu graciously accepted defeat in trying to find the base of the pillar, Brahma lied and claimed he flew to the top. I might have been content to allow their bickering, but I couldn't abide his dishonesty then, just as I can't understand his strange attempts to make amends now. So I revealed myself to them—infinite power with no beginning or end.

Not unexpectedly, Vishnu is waiting for me in the astral plane. "Please take me into battle with you, Destroyer of Fear."

"We have to find the battle first," I say. A part of me still scans the astral plane for some clue to their whereabouts, but I know that I can't find Andhaka so easily. My thoughts turn back to Mount Kailash. There was no sign of a struggle, not a sound or a flash of divine light. I have to assume Parvati evaded Andhaka when he approached her. But where would she go?

The shelter, of course, where she knows I can find her. Andhaka can follow her there, though he can't harm any of the residents. Why didn't I place my protection on the place itself? More to the point, why didn't I place my protection on Parvati herself?

With a roar that summons my army, I descend upon the shelter. Vishnu and Nandi answer my call first. Trident in hand, I charge the demons surrounding Parvati's shelter, reducing them to ash. It quiets the screams coming from the shelter, where my beloved calms the frightened humans within. At least I know she's safe.

Andhaka, hiding behind his minions, quakes when he sees me. A powerful throw flings my trident into his chest, splattering a thousand drops of blood. They touch the ground and more demons spawn from each droplet. As the demon horde converges on my army, I lose sight again of Andhaka. Fury ignites my blood. How dare this demon terrorize these downtrodden souls? How dare he threaten my goddess, the other half of my soul?

My palm slaps the drum I hold, and my feet respond to the vibrating rhythm with a memory older than time. One full stomp, then the ball of my foot taps the ground, followed by the heel. I lift the heel and stomp the ground again, with precision borne of long hours of meditation and control. After all, I can destroy the universe with a single misstep in my dance. Right now, I only need to clear away all these demons. Those four rhythmic beats are all it takes.

Nandi orders my army around the shelter, seeking out any stragglers or escapees, while Vishnu follows me through the doors. Everything is silent within ... too quiet, given what just occurred outside.

Vishnu's ever-spinning disc—a weapon of unmatched power in any world—eviscerates Andhaka's minions as we move silently through the rooms. Vishnu always was a skilled warrior, from the moment he broke the bow as Rama that allowed him to marry Sita, to the sheer strength needed for the child Krishna to uproot a pair of thousand-year-old trees when the barrel his mother bound him to stuck between them. Fighting at the Preserver's side all but assures victory.

I pierce other demon spawn with my trident, yanking away viciously as their bodies thump to the ground. The satisfying sound makes my toes twitch, but now is not the moment to dance.

We reach the door of Parvati's office and exchange glances when we hear Parvati's voice. I kick in the locked door, finding Andhaka pushing her down onto the sofa. His eyes linger on her chest, and his fingers inch toward his belt. I see red. More demons pack the space between them and us.

"... it is true," Parvati repeats, not for the first time, even as she fends him off. I can guess what she's been telling him. "You were born of my body like Ganesha was."

How can Parvati be so truthful and precise with her words in a moment like this? For she shaped Ganesha with her hands like a sculptor working clay. Andhaka, too, came to life from the literal sweat of her hands.

Andhaka still scoffs, unable to believe her because he can't see her for who she truly is.

These thoughts cross my mind in an instant while I charge forward.

Vishnu's disc cuts through the air before me. He decapitates the demon minions surrounding the couch, the weapon blurring with its speed. My trident impales, thrusts, and flings more bodies than should have fit in Parvati's office. Beside me, Vishnu fights with a ferocity few believe he possesses. But blood continues to fall from Andhaka's body. He should be weak by now, but I remember Brahma's promise to Andhaka. Only I can kill him. We slay the demons spawning from his dripping wound as we close in on them.

"Check on the residents," I tell Vishnu. Fire burns in Parvati's eyes as she fights back, but she doesn't shift forms until she sees Vishnu running for the stairs. Even now—when she faces mortal danger—she won't chance one of the people under her protection seeing her godly power.

If he possessed any sense, Andhaka would have been awestruck by my goddess as Kali shoves him off her. I admire her enough for the both of us. Black hair streaming loose behind her, wild and bloodshot eyes glaring from her sunken cheeks, fangs glistening against her blood-red lips, she is chaos incarnate. Her prayer necklace of demon skulls, her skirt of ... human arms for the absolution she offers her devotees, this version of my goddess is power, death, and destruction. She is glorious.

Kali toys with her prey, using her curved sword to draw more blood from Andhaka. But she laps up the spray of blood before it falls to the ground.

Clever.

"Why can't I have her?" Andhaka shrieks at me as he fends her off. "A beautiful woman, doomed to serve a charlatan snake-charmer on a mountain in the middle of nowhere. I could give her riches beyond compare, pleasure, and beautiful things. I'd show her off to the world. She appeared out of nowhere, with power and money enough for us to combine forces and take over the world. She has the kinds of gifts I have. We should be together. You have nothing compared to me. You'd keep her to yourself."

Andhaka's logic, such as it is, might make a twisted sort of sense if he actually understood who Parvati is. Instead, he believes that she—like Andhaka—comes of magical origins with no goals other than self-indulgence and power. Were they alike in that way, then they probably would have gravitated toward one another. Obviously, I would not have barred their path, nor might such a woman reject Andhaka's advances. But my beloved, who birthed this demon after a fashion, disavows all the things that Andhaka values. She will—and does—choose me in every life and every universe.

Of course someone who can only see my outward shape might assume some ... unflattering things about me. Matted hair coiled into a horn atop my head, ash smeared into my body, an ancient tiger skin draped around my waist, a serpent wound about my neck, lean muscles from untold millennia of meditation and yoga.

Andhaka cannot see the moon shining on my forehead, the river goddess Ganga winding through my hair, or the divine form of the snake god Vasuki. He doesn't see my third eye. He doesn't know the power I possess, the destruction I can wage without the strict discipline I've cultivated over eons of deprivation and loneliness. He only sees the ascetic. He is blind.

"How did you kill my general? He's twice your size, the most powerful of my fighters. Why are you so determined to stand in my way?" He's raving now, desperate to blame me for the circumstances of his own making.

Where do I even start? His true nature means that he twists everything into something vile. "A person isn't an object you can possess." I sigh, realizing I'm about to waste my breath with explanations he refuses to hear. "You tried to harm my beloved. And *she* is the Great Goddess. I do not control her actions. She is with me by her own choice."

Perhaps in another of Andhaka's reincarnations, my hand will slip on my trident and I'll touch his skin to burn away his sins. Maybe he will beg my forgiveness and I'll offer him mercy. Maybe I'll impale him on my trident and hold him there for a thousand years, until his body is nothing but a skeleton. But not today.

Kali steps away, recognizing my intent. I once prostrated myself before her to stop her killing, but she does not need such a reminder today. I blink open my third eye, its force concentrated on a single target.

Awareness—realization—flashes across Andhaka's face as the full import of Brahma's words finally sinks in. He recognizes me for who I truly am. But for him, in this incarnation at least, it is too late. Andhaka burns to ash. I take a careful breath, closing my destructive eye before I cause any further harm.

Parvati smiles at me, all traces of Kali gone. Nothing stands between us now, and she knows it as well as I do.

"It's so hot when you do that," Parvati murmurs, winding her arms around my neck.

I stifle a laugh at her attempt to act like a leering adolescent. With her breath hot against my lips and her curves pressing against my flesh, words little matter. She pulls herself up so she can wrap her legs around my hips. Her welcome weight reminds me of an eternity of other times we have joined like this, of the waiting eternity of times I still have with my beloved, either in this universe or the next.

"No wonder your devotees worship this," she teases, thrusting against me, our garments discarded. "I know I want to."

She's wrong: they worship the both of us in our union, the yoni and the lingam, two halves of one whole.

But we do anyway. And it—she—is divine.

Author Notes

If you enjoyed "Blind," please leave a review. Reviews help readers find new stories and guide writers to improve their craft.

In no particular order, I would like to thank

Anita Kharbanda, the most efficient critique partner ever,

Jennifer Moreland, without whom I would have mislabeled the yoga pose in the very first line,

Sapna Shah, for her vital feedback on the villain's character arc,

And, as always, my husband for putting up with my scribbling and offering constructive criticism. Thank you for believing in my dreams.

The 58-foot tall Azhimala Shiva statue, whose image appears on the cover, is located in Vizhinjam, Thiruvananthapuram, in Kerala, India. It was sculpted of concrete over a six-year period by the artist PS Devadathan. Per the artist, a sculpture of Nandi will eventually join Lord Shiva.

In "Blind," I have tried to stay faithful to the events of known Hindu mythology. Obviously this story is only a small sampling of the vast literature dedicated to Lord Shiva.

Many scholars attribute the variation in Hindu myths to reincarnation. Each different outcome in the mythology is said to originate from a different incarnation of the universe. This explanation satisfies all of my beliefs and questions as a practicing Hindu of Indian origin.

While popularly accepted Hindu mythology does not take place in the current day, "Blind" is my interpretation of the Hindu gods in the present.

My intent in writing this story was to explore the emotions of a deity who has existed—alone—across all universes and across all time. Many of the stories of Lord Shiva show him to flaunt conventional social mores and depict him as an outsider to what some consider traditional Hindu beliefs. A feminist, an ascetic, a hedonist—Lord Shiva encompasses many opposites. Trying to capture these many traits made writing "Blind" a fascinating challenge.

No disrespect to religion, culture, or anyone's beliefs was intended. Any errors in the story, whether of content or grammar, are my own. "Blind" is not to be taken as a fixed or final statement on Hinduism.

If you are interested in better understanding Hinduism, which is one of the oldest religions in the world, I urge you to do your own research across many different sources, as you may find conflicting information.

About the Author

Inspired by her South Asian roots and her lifelong fascination with magical worlds in fiction, Marah Devi writes diverse fantasy and fantasy romance.

When Marah tired of reading fantasy novels with no diversity, she took it upon herself to tell stories with sexy, multicultural heroes and strong female leads in unexpected settings.

Sign up for her newsletter at
http://teacuppublishing.com/marahdevi
to hear about upcoming releases and to receive exclusive content.

Marah Devi is the pen name for Preeti C. Sharma's adult romance and fantasy romance books.

You can expect more strong, smart heroines and swoon-worthy heroes that fall for them.

With an emphasis on diverse characters and cultures, Marah Devi's books will take you on sweeping adventures in worlds not commonly explored in Western fiction.

Happy endings after challenging trials ... love found amidst difficulty ... the ultimate victory of good over evil .... These form the basis of Marah's sexy fantasy stories.

Marah's books include the short story, "Blind," and the reverse-harem fantasy romance trilogy, "Beyond the Fae Veil."

Looking for another mermaid story? Check out

Redeeming the Demon's Daughter

The mermaid Suvarnamatsya and her clan-sisters live an idyllic life on the coast bordering her uncle's kingdom. Safe from war and any who might think her kind to be monsters, Suvi has known nothing but the security and privilege that comes of being a princess.

But when Hanuman, general of the god-king Rama's army, tries to build a bridge to Sri Lanka to face off against the demon-king Ravana, the mermaids' peace is shattered.

As Hanuman prepares to attack her father, Suvi can no longer avoid taking sides in this epic war between Rama and Ravana. She and her sisters sabotage the bridge's construction, opening themselves to the wrath of Rama's devotees.

Hanuman investigates the reason for the delayed construction and confronts his most unlikely adversary, a lovely mermaid who happens to be the daughter of his sworn enemy. Their fateful meeting challenges Suvi's beliefs—those of love, family loyalty, duty, godliness, and, most of all, redemption.

Suvi's choices and her ultimate sacrifice take her on a heart-rending journey from the coast of India to the feet of the gods.

Find out what happens to Suvi in this dramatic short story retelling from the Hindu epic, the Ramayana.

Get your copy of *Redeeming the Demon's Daughter* now!

OTHER WORKS BY THE AUTHOR

Books by Marah Devi

Blind

Beyond the Fae Veil

Books by Preeti C. Sharma

Blind (writing as Marah Devi)

Sea Deception
Sea Dreams
Sea Rivals
Sea Memories

Redeeming the Demon's Daughter

The Palace of the Two Towers

Free Worvanz
Dark Empire

Five Minutes at Hotel Stormcove
(an Atthis Arts Anthology)
A Step Through Time

Made in the USA
Columbia, SC
03 June 2022